Bonga Monga
in Hawaii

www.BongaMonga.com

WinePress Publishing (PO Box 428, Enumclaw, WA 98022) functions only as book publisher. As such, the ultimate design, content, editorial accuracy, and views expressed or implied in this work are those of the author.

ISBN 13: 978-1-60615-039-9
ISBN 10: 1-60615-039-1
Library of Congress Catalog Card Number: 2008900118

Printed in China.
APC-FT042001

The Travels of BongaMonga

in Hawaii

Written by Kay Perry
Illustrated By Darren Hassin

WinePress WP Publishing Kids

Bonga Monga sits in a taxi cab.

The cab stops and Bonga Monga
grabs the bags.

She runs to the check in desk.

She is glad.

Step. Step. Step.

Bonga Monga steps on to a big jet and sits.

**Bonga Monga has a cup of milk and a
fat yellow banana. It is fun.**

The fast jet lands in Hawaii.

Bonga Monga must get to the exit and step off the jet.

Step. Step. Step.

Bonga Monga steps on to a bus.

A man helps with Bonga Monga's bags.

The bus stops at the Hi·bis·cus Inn.

Bonga Monga grabs the bags and steps off of the bus.

Step. Step. Step.

The Hi·bis·cus Inn is grand.

Bonga Monga hums a song.

Bonga Monga has a sand·wich with jam, a sal·ad and a mango drink at the Banana Bon Bon Deli.

Then she puts on a hat and sun·glasses.

Step. Step. Step.

Bonga Monga steps on to the bus.

The bus stops at the forest.

Step. Step. Step.

Bonga Monga steps on the wet path.

Bonga Monga jumps and swings
on the big plants.

Swing, swing, swing.

A grass hut sits on top of a hill.

Step. Step. Step.

Bonga Monga steps into the hut.

Bonga Monga sits on a pink rug with
black dots and sips a lemon drink.

It is fun.

Step. Step. Step.

Can Bonga Monga jump up
on a banana plant?

Bonga Monga gets to a big plant.

Nuts hang from its branches. Not bananas.

She is not sad. Bonga Monga runs on.

At last Bonga Monga is at a banana plant.

Lots of bananas hang from the plant.

Step. Step. Step. Jump. Jump. Swing. Swing.

She picks a banana.

Bonga Monga munches a big yellow banana.

Yum. She fills a bag with bananas.

It is dusk.

Bonga Monga blinks at the pink sunset.

She stops. It is mag·ni·fi·cent.

Step, step, step went Bonga Monga.

Squish, squish, squish went
Bonga Monga's flip flops.

The bus sits at the end of the path.

Bonga Monga hands the man
the big bag of bananas.

Then she step, step, steps up on the bus.

The bus passes lots of in·te·rest·ing things.

Bonga Monga is glad she had
such a fan·tas·tic trip.

Fun and snacks

Sun and sand

Let us give thanks

This land is grand.

Aloha